Dear Parent:

Congratulations! Your child is taking the first steps on an exciting journey. The destination? Independent reading!

STEP INTO READING® will help your child get there. The program offers books at five levels that accompany children from their first attempts at reading to reading success. Each step includes fun stories, fiction and nonfiction, and colorful art. There are also Step into Reading Sticker Books, Step into Reading Math Readers, Step into Reading Write-In Readers, Step into Reading Phonics Readers, and Step into Reading Phonics First Steps! Boxed Sets—a complete literacy program with something to interest every child.

Learning to Read, Step by Step!

Ready to Read Preschool–Kindergarten
• big type and easy words • rhyme and rhythm • picture clues
For children who know the alphabet and are eager to begin reading.

Reading with Help Preschool–Grade 1
• basic vocabulary • short sentences • simple stories
For children who recognize familiar words and sound out new words with help.

Reading on Your Own Grades 1–3
• engaging characters • easy-to-follow plots • popular topics
For children who are ready to read on their own.

Reading Paragraphs Grades 2–3
• challenging vocabulary • short paragraphs • exciting stories
For newly independent readers who read simple sentences with confidence.

Ready for Chapters Grades 2–4
• chapters • longer paragraphs • full-color art
For children who want to take the plunge into chapter books but still like colorful pictures.

STEP INTO READING® is designed to give every child a successful reading experience. The grade levels are only guides. Children can progress through the steps at their own speed, developing confidence in their reading, no matter what their grade.

Remember, a lifetime love of reading starts with a single step!

For Ramona

Educators and librarians, for a variety of teaching tools, visit us at
www.randomhouse.com/teachers

www.randomhouse.com/kids/disney
www.stepintoreading.com

Library of Congress Cataloging-in-Publication Data
Jordan, Apple.
  Just like me! / by Apple Jordan.
    p. cm. — (Step into reading. Step 1)
  Summary: Roo becomes friends with a Heffalump named Lumpy and learns that they are very much alike after all.
  ISBN 0-7364-2288-9 (pbk.) – ISBN 0-7364-8039-0 (lib. bdg.)
  [1. Fear–Fiction. 2. Friendship–Fiction.] I. Title. II. Series.
  PZ7.J755 Ju 2005
  [E]–dc22
  2004003801

Printed in the United States of America 10 9 8 7 6 5 4 3 2

STEP INTO READING®

STEP 1

Walt Disney
PICTURES PRESENTS

Pooh's
Heffalump
MOVIE

Just Like Me

By Apple Jordan

Illustrated by the Disney Storybook Artists

Designed by Disney Publishing's Global Design Group

Random House 🏠 New York

Kanga and Roo

hear a strange sound.

Ta-root! Ta-root!

What can it be?

Roo finds
a footprint.

Rabbit says

it must be a heffalump.

"What is a heffalump?"
asks Roo.

"A heffalump is scary!"
says Tigger.

But Roo wants

to find a heffalump.

Roo catches a heffalump.

His name is Lumpy.

But Lumpy is not scary.
Lumpy is just like Roo.

Lumpy likes

to run and play . . .

. . . just like Roo.

Lumpy likes

to make a mess . . .

. . . just like Roo.

Lumpy likes

tasty snacks . . .

. . . just like Roo.

And Lumpy likes
to splash . . .

. . . just like Roo.

Roo lets Lumpy go.

Now they are friends.

Roo takes Lumpy home
to meet his friends.

His friends are scared.

They catch Lumpy.

"Lumpy is not scary," says Roo.

"Lumpy is just like us!"

Mama heffalumps
are just like us, too.

They love

their babies . . .

. . . just as Kanga
loves Roo!